Wonder World KiDS

THE CASE OF THE
LOST
LLAMAS

Book 2

Written by Dori Marx

Illustrated by Priscila Orozco Gallo

ISBN: 978-1-7323424-1-5

For all my animal friends who touched
our souls in passing or left a permanent
imprint on our hearts – D.M.

CHAPTER 1

"Hey, droopy, wake up! We're getting ready to land!" Eight-year-old Fynn Cook was rudely shaken awake by his twin sister. In his dream, he had just crossed the finish line of his first running race, a 5K. The cheers of the crowd were ringing in his ears, and he could still feel the ground under his sneakers.

Fynn sleepily raised his head, which was resting against the plane window. Before he fell asleep, he had boarded a plane with his parents and two sisters on its way to the country of **Peru** in South America. Fynn yawned, tousled his short blond hair with his fingers, and looked over the aisle.

The Doctors Cook were deep in thought, bent over paper files that had been sent to them in preparation for their next mysterious case. Fynn's parents were two of the world's most well-known veterinarians.

They specialized in strange illnesses and were called in to solve animal-related problems all around the earth.

Fynn and his sisters, Celia and Lilly, were lucky to go with them on their trips whenever they were not in school.

Actually, my parents are the lucky ones, thought Fynn. The Cook kids were expert animal mystery solvers themselves. They had helped their parents crack a difficult case more than once.

Ten-year-old Lilly would probably agree with her little brother on this. Currently, her long blond hair framed her face as she crouched over her phone. She was using the time on the plane to research the native animals of their new destination: Peru. So far, she had discovered many **camelid** species, some of which she wasn't familiar with. She had seen a **llama** and an **alpaca** of course. *But what would a **vicuña** look like?* she wondered.

After having successfully woken her twin brother, Celia Cook turned back to the monitor. She was watching their flight path closely. It felt like they had spent days on the plane, and she was ready to arrive. Ready to find out about the llamas and what was bothering those cute, furry animals.

Across from Celia, her mom packed away the charts and papers and said,

"Well, this was part one of our journey. I'm afraid we'll have a couple more stops before arriving at **Machu Picchu,** the home of the lost llamas."

Celia groaned. "More stops, Mom? Are you serious?"

Fynn looked out of the window again and whispered the words that sounded like a magic spell: *Machu Picchu.*

CHAPTER 2

"So let me get this straight..." For what seemed like the past ten hours Celia had bombarded her parents with impatient questions. Currently, she stood on the platform of a simple looking train station, her little suitcase next to her, and glared up at her parents.

"First, we took the plane to Lima, the capital of Peru. Then, we boarded another small plane to a city in the mountains, Cuzco. Afterward, we sat on a train for hours travelling through the valleys. And now you're telling me that this isn't that Maeshyou Peeshyou place either?" Celia gestured impatiently around her and covered her face with her hands.

Fynn had spent the long trip pulling up information about their final destination. He laughed and corrected his twin, "When we finally arrive, you might want to be able to pronounce the place correctly, right? It's called 'maaachoo peechoo' like you would sneeze and put an *M* and a *Pee* in front of it. Try it!"

Their big sister Lilly joined him in practicing the sounds. Soon all three Cook kids were happily sneezing and coughing Machu Picchu sounding noises until their bellies hurt.

"The name actually means 'Old Mountain' in the **Quechua** language, so that's where we've got to go next," said Fynn, pointing up to one of the high peaks around the train station.

"The **Incas,** the tribe that lived here until about five hundred years ago, built their cities high up in the mountains. They used the great volcanic soil to grow food and stayed well-hidden and protected up there," said Fynn, sharing his discoveries with his sisters.

During his short research about the Incas, he had already become fascinated by these strong people. *What a fantastic strategy to make your home high up in the mountains,* he thought.

Fynn tried to picture the effort it had taken to bring materials, animals, and people up those peaks without the help of trucks or tractors.

And here was Celia complaining about her tired ballerina toes. All they had to do was step off a plane onto a train and now continue onto a comfortable bus. Fynn cast a glance over at his twin, who had gone back to arguing with their tired looking parents.

At that moment, the Cook family was interrupted by the noisy arrival of a rusty looking smoking vehicle on the other side of the platform. It looked like a bus all right but certainly not the comfortable kind that Fynn had pictured them boarding a minute ago. He took a deep breath and stepped onto the bus, ready for the last part of their travels.

Celia was ready to finally arrive somewhere, too. Her tablet with her ballet recital music had run out of battery what seemed like ages ago. She was also way past the stage of finding interesting things outside the windows of the various modes of transportation they had taken so far.

Nothing, however, could have prepared her or her siblings for what came next. The shaking bus began to move forward and immediately upward. The kids were pressed back into their seats and thrown left, bumping into each other. Celia clamped her arms around Lilly and looked out of the dusty window.

This can't be happening, Celia thought. The bus chugged at an impossible angle on a dusty, narrow road winding left and right and left again.

"I'm starting to see why none of the Inca cities got attacked up there. At this rate, I'm not sure we'll ever make it to Machu Picchu alive," she whispered to Lilly as she held on for dear life.

CHAPTER 3

Although they were all still breathing when the bus stopped, Celia felt barely alive when she climbed down the steps on shaking legs.

"What in the world was that?" said Lilly, jumping out of the bus after her.

"I know!" said Fynn, following them out onto the dusty road. "Wasn't this the most amazing ride ever?"

"Well, I'm not entirely sure, that's what I'd call it," said their mom, dusting off her khaki pants.

"How about that time when the other bus going downhill tried to pass us, Mom? I thought this was a one-lane road, but those buses made it work somehow, squeezing by. I swear I was holding my breath and looking down at certain death on my side," said Fynn, all pumped up.

"I swear I'll throw up if you continue talking!" growled Celia at her brother.

Their twin fight was stopped by a young boy, who ran toward the Cook family while wildly waving his long arms.

"Bienvenidos!" he shouted as soon as he came to a sliding stop next to them.

"Me llamo, Maximo," said the boy. "I'm Maximo. My mom sent me to meet you here. She was held up at the ruins.

 Everyone is so busy looking for the llamas. I hope you can help us! Are you tired? You look tired! We have a special room for you at the Sanctuary. Are you hungry? You look hungry! We have food for you at the Sanctuary. Do you need to..."

The boy kept firing questions and answers at them in a long, never-ending stream of words. Fynn was flabbergasted by this rapid welcome.

Everything about the boy looked fast: he was tall and fit, like a marathon runner, his long arms moved up and down in rhythm with the crazy amount of words, and even his dark, curly locks bounced along. *What a strange boy,* thought Fynn. *I can't wait to get to know his story.*

Lilly and Celia giggled as soon as their host had spoken his very first words.

"Your name is Maximo?" Lilly's question interrupted him quite rudely.

"Si! Yes!" said the boy.

"That's so funny! I can't believe it!" said Celia, hopping up and down and shaking her head in disbelief.

Maximo stopped moving and looked at the girls, puzzled.

"It's only..." Lilly had a hard time controlling her laughter. "We just came from another case. We helped a boy called Max save his dancing horses in Vienna," she finally said.

"Max and Maximo? I see! I guess, we're making it easy for you to remember our names, right?" said Maximo, laughing as well. He led them away from the dust of the bus stop, up the stairs of the building he had called the Sanctuary.

The boy took them through the lobby to a sunny patio in the back of the building.

Fynn immediately ran up to the rough stone wall at the edge. Stretched below them were the ancient ruins of Machu Picchu. The city was so much bigger than he had imagined. Paths wound their ways up and down the mountains. Ruins of large stone buildings were scattered all over, guarded by walls and gates.

"Everything's made of stone!" he marveled.

"Yes, the Incas were famous for their stone work. It was almost like modern masonry. Even without all our new tools, they shaped the rocks to fit perfectly. You'll see when we get closer and walk the ruins tomorrow," said Maximo.

Tomorrow! Fynn yawned. It felt like he would need all his energy back to walk those steep stony paths on the lookout for Maximo's llamas.

CHAPTER 4

In the morning, the Cook family joined Maximo and his mother, Mrs. Curador, in a large dining room decorated with colorful Inca shawls.

"It's so good to finally meet you, **Señora** Curador!" said Mrs. Cook, shaking the woman's hand. "Maximo was the perfect host welcoming us. We heard you ran into some trouble at the ruins yesterday?"

It was easy to see that Mrs. Curador and Maximo were mother and son. Her pitch-black hair bounced in wild ringlets around her head, and she had the same happy dark eyes as her son. While she spoke, her hands rapidly moved through the air.

"We're so glad that you have made the long journey to us," she said, embracing Mrs. Cook warmly.

Fynn winked at Celia. *At least someone is glad about the long journey,* he mocked her silently.

"I'm afraid your work is getting more urgent by the minute. Our tourists are angry. The other caretakers don't have answers. We desperately need the help of the Doctors Cook here!" Mrs. Curador said.

Lilly saw her parents exchange worried glances. They knew that running the day-to-day work in the ancient city was a big job for an **anthropologist** such as Maximo's mom. She protected and studied the old Inca ruins. She also had to keep all the current visitors and tourists happy.

Her younger siblings seemed undisturbed by these difficult problems. The twins were busy stuffing various delicious breakfast items into their mouths. Celia went for a second serving of a hot, creamy soup. Fynn had already

collected a platter full of fried **plantains,** which he dipped in honey.

"Are you guys even listening?" hissed Lilly.

"Oh relax, Lilly!" said Celia. "We'll get to the bottom of the llama problem soon enough. You know we can't think on an empty stomach."

Or full stomach or tired feet or too much noise or too little sleep... Lilly continued the mental list before turning back to the conversation her parents were having with Mrs. Curador.

"As I was telling you," Lilly heard her say, "our llamas simply stopped coming

to the ruins three weeks ago. We've tried everything at this point. My team can't locate them on any of the mountains."

"How many animals are we talking about?" asked Mrs. Cook.

"Before they went missing, we had two dozen llamas in total. Each of them has a name tag in its ear. One of my favorites is called Lily," said Maximo, smiling at the human Lily next to him.

A llama Lily! Now Lily was even more determined to find those poor missing animals as soon as possible.

"Although they walk freely around the summit and through the ruins, the llamas always meet in a certain grassy spot in the morning. They're predictable animals. Our llamas also use some of the old Inca fountains as watering holes. I can't even imagine where they'll find clean water close by," said Mrs. Curador.

Fynn shuddered. It sounded like something terrible had happened to the llamas to disrupt their daily routine.

"What makes matters worse is that our visitors have started asking about the missing llamas. The Internet is buzzing with questions and theories. We can't have tourists searching the grounds for clues. We can't ignore their questions.

It's an impossible situation for us," said Mrs. Curador, sighing deeply.

"We really depend on **tourism** up here to have money for our research. There's still so much to learn about the Incas and their **civilization**," said Maximo in a lower voice to the children next to him.

Celia slurped the last of her soup thoughtfully. She was ready to help their new friend. She was excited to walk the ruins looking for Lily, the llama. At the same time, she made a mental note to sneak off to the kitchen later. Her mission now also included finding out the secret of the mouthwatering soup she just had eaten for breakfast.

CHAPTER 5

Shortly afterward, the Cook family and their hosts took off toward the entrance to the ruins of Machu Picchu. The large gates were just a couple of steps from the Sanctuary, where they had spent the night and enjoyed their breakfast.

"I'm really glad we could have you up here at the hotel for your stay," said Mrs. Curador. "The Sanctuary is the only place to sleep on the mountain. Everyone else must arrive in the morning on the bus you took yesterday. The early morning is the time we can walk the city in peace and quiet."

Celia looked at their host thankfully. She sure was glad she wasn't expected to go on the nail-biting journey on the rusty old bus every morning during their stay.

The guards at the gates were busy with their morning preparations getting the long ticket lines ready for the visitors. When they saw Mrs. Curador and Maximo, they all smiled and waved the small group through. The Cook family entered through the wide gates to the ancient ruins of Machu Picchu.

After passing the first bend of a narrow cobblestone path, the entire magnificent sight came into view. They looked down onto small fields of green grass, borders of stone walls, arches made out of nothing but rocks, and buildings of every shape and size. The Incas had fitted the ancient city of Machu Picchu neatly into the mountain.

The entire city was following the landscape up and down in a natural way. Snowy mountain peaks and white clouds surrounded the scene like the frame of a painting.

"Everything is so straight, so geometrical," said Lilly.

"It looks like a hidden city in the clouds," said Celia at the same time.

"You're both right!" said Mrs. Curador. "The Inca king **Pachacuti** chose not only the prettiest but also the safest spot for his city. Nobody can see the location looking up from the valley. And yes, Lilly. The Incas were amazing engineers, even back in the year 1450 when this city was built."

"Do you kids see the terraces down there?" asked Mr. Cook.

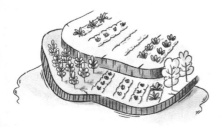

"The things that look like giant green steps from up here, Dad?" asked Fynn.

35

"Yes," said Mr. Cook smiling. "The Inca engineers created those 'steps' along the mountainside and filled them with rich earth to plant their crops. Corn, potatoes, and beans all grew up here back then."

"And they had llama herds," said Maximo. "Llamas helped them with carrying heavy stuff, and their poop made the ground better for planting."

"Natural fertilizer!" said Lilly. "The Incas were not only great builders but smart farmers as well."

"Let's walk down a little farther. I want to show you the amazing stone creations up close," said Mrs. Curador.

CHAPTER 6

They continued their journey into the city. The Incas had built stone paths winding up and down the mountain, so it was a smooth walk. There was, however, an endless looking number of steps. The children and their parents gladly stopped to catch their breaths when Mrs. Curador pointed to something along the way.

Fynn realized that Maximo had no need to stop. While they were looking at buildings, he hopped up and down the steps around them, his dark curls bouncing.

"All the beautiful stones around you were cut and shaped without any real tools. The Incas chipped them by hand," said Mrs. Curador.

The kids were speechless. The large stones, some of them even bigger than the three siblings, were smooth and fit perfectly together.

Rocks all around them created straight walls and curved arches. Fynn knew how difficult it was to chip away exact pieces from a stone. Sometimes he pretended to mine for jewels with the rocks in his yard. *I have never ever managed to shape a rock like that!* he thought.

They had now crossed the entire city and climbed higher again until they were standing on a flat, grassy area. It showed a magnificent view of the ruins below. Fynn looked all around in wonder, then his eyes glanced down at the grass by his feet. He was standing next to a bunch of scattered brown beans.

"Llama poop!" he shouted happily.

"This is their usual hangout," said Maximo.

Mrs. Curador and the doctors walked around discussing details, pointing to the ground here and there. Maximo took the siblings to the edge of the field.

"Our llamas could be anywhere," he said sadly, facing the high peaks around them. "I just hope they're ok."

Fynn looked at the city in the clouds just below him. He couldn't understand how a large group of  animals could suddenly vanish from up here. *Did they just take off and look for a new home? Did someone kidnap them?* Suddenly, he saw movement farther down the hill. *Could that be the herd of llamas?*

"It looks like the main gates just opened," said Mrs. Curador, walking toward them. "I'm afraid our time alone is over."

She wasn't joking! A large dark mass moved up the main path below, splitting into smaller groups and filling the lower part of the city within minutes.

The visitors look like an ant invasion from up here, Lilly thought before turning away and following her family.

On their way back, the main gates of Machu Picchu reminded them of the entrance to Disney World. Person after person jumped out of the dusty busses, some of them looking as nauseous as Celia had been, but all of them hurrying on to enter their final destination.

CHAPTER 7

Lilly let out a deep exhale when they escaped into the lobby of the hotel and closed the doors behind them. *Now I know why they decided to name the only hotel up here the Sanctuary,* she thought.

"The ruins are out-of-this-world beautiful and unique. I get why everyone wants to travel to see them. But how on earth do you deal with all these tourists every day?" said Celia.

Maximo sighed. Celia and her family were one of the lucky few to have seen the ancient city of Machu Picchu as it was meant to be, without too many people around.

"So, Maximo," said Fynn, interrupting the gloomy thoughts, "I saw you running up and down those steps before."

"Yes, I really enjoy running on the Inca trails," said Maximo. "It's a great challenge to keep your balance and speed on the rocky paths."

Fynn nodded. "See, I'm signed up

to run my first race soon. I actually should be training  right now. When we get back home, I'll only have a little more time to prepare. So, I was wondering. Would you be able to train with me?"

"And maybe give you some running advice? Yes?" asked Maximo.

Fynn shrugged. "Why not? If I'll end up running up and down without being out of breath just like you, I'll take all your advice," he said.

Lilly had stayed close to her parents and Mrs. Curador. After this morning's walk on the mountain, she was growing more and more worried about the missing llamas. And especially Lily the llama!

"As our first step, we'll set up food stations all around the natural borders of the city. Nothing fancy, just a couple of treats that would attract the llamas," her mom explained.

"They really like sliced sweet potatoes, carrots, and apples," said Mrs. Curador.

"Lilly and I can go to the kitchen and prepare some bowls of those treats for them," said Celia, who had not forgotten about her other quest. She was excited to have an excuse for visiting the kitchen.

"Perfect!" said her mom. "Your dad and I will walk back to the ruins to pick a couple of spots for our experiment. Hopefully, the treats will get the herd out of hiding, and we'll be able to follow their tracks back to their secret location."

If they are hiding, thought Lilly sadly. She really hoped nothing worse had happened to the llama herd.

"Come on, Lilly!" said Celia, who was on a mission now. "We'll head to the kitchen right away."

"I'll join Mom and Dad on the mountain," said her twin. "Maximo promised to train with me for my race. Man, is he fast! If I can learn his secret,

I'll bring home the gold!" Fynn pumped his fists in the air and took off to change into his running gear.

"Oh boy!" said Lilly and Celia, looking at each other.

CHAPTER 8

The hotel kitchen was a busy world of colors, smells, and sounds. Celia and Lilly entered timidly. They were welcomed by a booming voice.

"Bienvenidos!" An enormous man with a towering chef's hat came toward them. He wiped his giant hands on his dirty apron, which hadn't been white for a long time. The sisters gasped and took a step back.

"Welcome to my kitchen! I'm Chef **Cuchillo.** You can call me Chef Chuchu. Señora Curador called to tell us you were coming. You're interested in my cooking?" said the giant man. Up close, he had a warm smile and friendly eyes that twinkled under his bushy eyebrows.

Celia relaxed and inhaled. *Everything in this kitchen smells heavenly,* she thought. Then she remembered her manners and stretched out her hand toward Chef Chuchu.

"Buenos dias! My name is Celia, and this is my sister, Lilly. We travelled here with our parents from the United States. I loved your breakfast this morning! Do you think I'll be able to cook your chicken soup at home?" she said quickly.

Chef Chuchu's face became even rounder as he smiled widely at Celia's words.

"Of course! Come here, my new junior cook in training!" he said to Celia, taking her hand and shaking it more gently than the girls had thought possible given his gigantic size.

Chef Chuchu and Celia spent the next hour discussing the best ingredients (fresh corn), his best kept secret (a squeeze of lime juice), and the best cooking method (slow simmer) to make his famous breakfast soup.

Since they had started to raise their own chickens at home, Lilly didn't want to eat chicken meat anymore. She wasn't a vegetarian yet, but it had become easy for her to say no to chicken meat.

Instead of cooking, Lilly busied herself with preparing the treat bowls for the llamas. After all, her parents were counting on their help.

One of the friendly kitchen helpers offered to show her the right bowls and where the fresh ingredients were kept. While they were working on preparing the first llama treat bowl, they all chatted. Lilly soon learned many interesting facts about the food, the hotel, and the ancient city.

The local people enjoyed a big lunch and an afternoon snack instead of eating a big dinner. The afternoon snack was called "lonche." This reminded Lilly a lot of the English word "lunch."

Chef Chuchu's life was tightly connected with the hotel that opened in the year 1947. He had been at the Sanctuary since he was a child and had experienced many changes in the hotel and on the mountain. In his stories, real tourism to Machu Picchu started only about twenty years ago.

"Before that, things were quieter and slower up here," he said. "Soon we'll have ten times as many visitors, more than one million people per year."

As Lilly chopped carrots, apples, and sweet potatoes, she thought about how different everything must have looked at that time. *Were there more llamas around then?* she wondered.

Her thoughts drifted to the lost herd. She pictured her soon-to-be friend Lily the llama, walking up to the treats and raising her soft brown eyes to gaze at her thankfully. Human Lilly was just reaching over to grab a handful of salad leaves to top off the last bowl when a high-pitched shriek sounded from the greens.

Curiously, Lilly took a step over and looked behind the salad dish. In the far corner of the counter was a small wire cage. As she leaned closer, two pairs of beady eyes looked back at her.

"Guinea pigs!" Lilly gasped in surprise. *What on earth are these two pets doing in the hotel kitchen?*

"Oh, I see you've found our next traditional dish. We call them **cuy**," said Chef Chuchu from across the room.

"We call them guinea pigs," said Lilly. "But wait... *dish?* What do you mean, Chef Chuchu?"

CHAPTER 9

Fynn and Maximo had made their way back to the ruins. They weaved their path through visitors taking pictures, posing for pictures, or listening to guides explaining the story of Machu Picchu.

"Hiram Bingham, a young professor from **Yale University,** found these ruins by accident in 1911. He was looking for a different lost city of the Incas when he stumbled upon Machu Picchu, overgrown by the jungle at that time. It was a lost city, nobody even knew that it existed," a guide explained to his group as Fynn walked by.

Fascinating, thought Fynn. His mind flashed to his favorite image of himself winning the gold medal at his race back home. Then he added on to his daydream: Maximo and he were standing next to a lost ruin with a golden arch glimmering in the sunshine.

His parents and Mrs. Curador beamed with pride. Newspaper headlines all over the world...

That Bingham guy came all the way from Yale, so he was almost Fynn's neighbor in Connecticut in the United States. *This can't be a coincidence, right?* Fynn grinned excitedly.

"Come on, Fynn!" called Maximo impatiently. "One of the less travelled Inca paths starts over there. Let's go where we can actually run."

Behind a small hill, they reached a trail paved with rough rocks. Fynn instantly recognized the work of the Inca engineers. "Where does this trail lead to?" he asked.

"It's just a small part of the Inca trail system. They built a large network of these roads and rope bridges all throughout the **Andes Mountains,** you know," explained Maximo.

"The Inca mailmen were called **chasquis;** you say it like 'tchas-kiss.' They were awesome runners who carried secret messages from one Inca town to the other. They blew a conch shell when they got close to the next runner, so he could prepare and start running right away. Chasquis had to be fast and accurate. If they messed up, they were killed by the king."

"No way!" said Fynn. *No wonder the Incas were great runners.*

The boys took off in a sprint and followed the ups and downs of the winding path. At first, Fynn struggled with the uneven paving. There were rocks sticking up out of the ground everywhere making him stumble. Soon, he was able to match Maximo's smooth pace and followed the local boy's steps. His body took over the rhythm of running; he was breathing in and out easily. In and out. In and out.

Fynn felt like he could run like this forever, and he let his thoughts wander. Fast Inca runners, secret messages, lost cities, and explorers... it was almost like he had been dropped into an adventure story in one of his books at home.

"Heya, boys!" they suddenly heard familiar voices calling and came to a stop.

Fynn and Maximo had been so lost in their running that they had not spotted their parents walking just ahead on a field next to the path. Instantly, Fynn felt a pang of remorse. Here he was out running and dreaming of adventures while his parents were working hard to find Maximo's llamas.

"Any luck, Mom?" he called out.

"Not yet," his mom said. "We're still not entirely sure what's going on. But we've got some good spots for our traps. Dad and I agree that the herd must have found some shelter to spend the nights. We'll try to place the treat bowls close to some rocky areas."

Fynn nodded. He remembered how his rescue goats had escaped a while ago. His family had moved the small herd to an overgrown part of their yard. Goats were amazing at eating invasive weeds. They enjoyed munching on plants that didn't belong in the area and that destroyed other useful plants.

Everything went well until a large falling branch spooked them. The goats jumped over their fence and took off running into the woods. Nobody could

chase them down, and the kids were worried for their safety all day long. Their parents had told them not to be scared.

And really! As soon as it got dark, the entire herd made its way back to their little barn. Fynn was the one who had found them before going to bed. The goats were lying on their straw beds and chewing their evening hay as if nothing had happened at all.

Hopefully, the llamas will act just like their goat relatives, thought Fynn. If they have looked for shelter, the chances of them being still close are good.

CHAPTER 10

"Mom! Dad!" Lilly and Celia came running as soon as Fynn entered the hotel with his parents. "They eat guinea pigs!" said Celia sobbing, and she threw herself into her mother's arms.

Fynn looked at Maximo in surprise, and his friend looked back at him equally surprised.

"You eat your pets?" asked Fynn.

"You don't eat cuy?" asked Maximo.

"Why don't we all sit down with a cup of hot cocoa and some picarones?" said Mr. Cook quickly. "Mrs. Curador tells me they taste even better than our doughnuts."

Soon everyone was seated comfortably back on the beautiful patio overlooking the ruins. The girls dug into plates of the delicious local doughnuts. Fynn finished his second cup of hot cocoa. He was tired from his first training with Maximo, but he also couldn't wait to hear what had upset his sisters.

"So, here I am, preparing some veggie and fruit treats for the llamas, when I hear some cute little squeaking. Behind me, I see two beautiful long-haired guinea pigs sitting in a cage in the kitchen. And then Chef Chuchu—who is as big as a bear but really nice—tells us they're breeding those two beauties because they actually eat roasted guinea pigs!"

"How can this be, Mom? I'm so disgusted!" said Lilly, finishing her story and scrunching up her entire face.

"That must have been such a shock, Lilly! I'm sorry, girls," said her mom, putting a hand on Lilly's arm. "We have to accept that different countries have different customs though. Some animals

are pets in one culture and food in another. You've heard about the sacred cows in India, for example. And we in America love our steaks and hamburgers, don't we?"

"True," said Lilly. "Still... it makes me sad and angry." *And I want to do something to help them,* she added quietly.

"Unfortunately, guinea pigs don't really exist in the wild anymore around here," explained her dad. "They are simply bred for their meat. Just like cows or pigs where we come from."

"I don't think I've ever thought of **cuyes** as pets before you brought it up," said Maximo, scratching his nose. "I even learned in school that their English name, guinea pig, might come from the European sailors comparing their meat to the roasting pigs that they ate back home. Cuy is really delicious. We only have them for special celebrations, and I've always looked forward to it. I'm sorry, guys!"

Not surprisingly, none of the explanations had calmed the girls. Both Celia and Lilly still looked freaked out.

Fynn understood Maximo's point of view, but he was also disturbed by the thought of eating a little pet. After all, guinea pigs were not that different from his sister's hamster back home. But he also knew that Lilly didn't eat chickens because they reminded her of their flock. At the same time, he had to admit that he loved some juicy chicken nuggets any time of day—even though he took care of the hens in their yard and had named quite a few of their chicks. *This whole food thing is just way too complicated to solve right away,* he decided.

"How about we focus on helping the animals we came here for?" said Mrs. Cook, reading his thoughts. "I'd like to take those treat bowls you girls prepared for the traps. Let's start setting them up around the city before it gets too late in the day."

"Ok, Mom. We'll all help," said Lilly. She put the picture of the sad little caged guinea pigs out of her mind but swore that she would do everything in her power to help them. Local dish or not, she could at least rescue these two cuyes while she was here.

CHAPTER 11

The next few hours were busy for everyone. The Cook family carried the food for the llamas to the places the doctors had found on their morning walk with Mrs. Curador. They made slow progress. Even this late in the afternoon, buses with visitors from the valley were still arriving. The small paths between the main parts of the ruins were crowded.

"Many people come up the mountain to see the sunset over the city," explained Maximo. "I can't blame them. It's a magical time of day."

"I sure can blame them. We'll never find the llamas if these people are constantly in our way," said Fynn in an annoyed voice. He had almost dropped his bowl again as a group of older couples carrying walking sticks bumped into him. Now Fynn was trying to pass a group of college kids striking silly poses in front of one of the large stone arches.

"Ouch!" screamed Celia. "Not again!"

Fynn looked over at his sister and saw her jumping up and down on one foot.

"They keep trampling my toes!" she explained.

Fynn motioned "sorry" with his hands. He knew how important Celia's precious ballet feet were to her.

"Almost there," said Mr. Cook. "We can place the last two bowls on the other side of this stone wall." He pointed to one of the terraces below them. "Fynn, why don't you and Maximo take them down and put one on each side. Let's give your sister's dancing toes a little rest before we have to make our way back." He winked at his twins.

The boys walked down the grassy field and jumped over the knee-high stone

wall while balancing the last two bowls of crunchy treats. Maximo pointed left, and Fynn nodded. He took his bowl and continued to the left along the wall while his friend headed right. When he thought he had walked far enough, he crouched down to find a good even spot for the bowl. Hopefully, the llamas would find it and have a little snack this evening.

As he straightened up again, something moved in a pile of rocks next to him. *It's too small to be a llama,* was Fynn's first thought. *Ridiculous.* He laughed. *Llamas don't hide under piles of rocks.* He moved closer to investigate.

In a little nook sat a medium-sized animal with gorgeous gray fur. It had small black eyes and large erect ears. Curious whiskers moved up and down as it looked back at Fynn. If it weren't for the long furry tail that was curling out of the wall, he would have thought it was a rabbit.

"Oh, you've found a **viscacha!**" said Maximo, who had sneaked up on him. "They're our, what do you call them, chinchillas?"

Fynn and the chinchilla were both startled by Maximo's voice, and the furry animal took off running.

"They live here in the wild?" asked Fynn, surprised.

"Yes," said Maximo. "It's really rare to spot them in the ruins with all the people walking around. You're lucky that you saw one."

The friends started to head back toward the rest of the group. Fynn felt they had made a lot of progress today. He had started training with Maximo, who was the fastest runner he had ever met. They had set food traps all around the border of the ancient ruins to attract the llamas. And now, he had even seen a wild chinchilla. He couldn't wait to tell Lilly about it. She would be so jealous that she had missed meeting a new animal!

CHAPTER 12

When Fynn woke up the next morning, the sun was already shining through the window, and the beds next to him were empty. He stretched his aching legs and hurried up to join his family in the dining room for breakfast.

Downstairs, Fynn found his sisters and Maximo crouched over some photographs spread on one of the tables.

83

"Where are Mom and Dad?" he asked them, yawning.

"They went out early this morning with Mrs. Curador to check on the traps," said his twin sister.

"How are your legs?" asked Maximo, grinning.

"Well, let's say I won't apply as an Inca mailman just yet," said Fynn and laughed. "Breakfast first!"

He went to grab a cup of orange juice and some more of those delicious fried plantains from the day before. Balancing the plate and glass, he joined his sisters and Maximo at the table.

"What are you guys looking at?" he asked.

"Maximo is showing us pictures of the herd," said Lilly. "Look, this is llama Lily! Her tag number in her ear is the twenty-three, see? Isn't she the cutest? I really want to find her today." Lilly pointed to a close-up of a hairy white face with huge watery eyes and two enormous buck-teeth pointing out of its hairy pursed lips.

"Looks like a Lilly to me!" said Fynn, laughing. *Cute* was definitely not the word he would use to describe this creature.

"Besides llamas, we also have alpacas and vicuñas. They're all members of the camelid family, just like camels. The vicuña is the national symbol of our country, Peru," said Maximo and pointed to another photograph. "These are the only ones that still live in herds in the wild. They're actually protected."

"Vicuñas look so delicate! Almost like small deer, right?" said Celia.

"Yes, they're the smallest. The llamas are the largest breed. They've been used as pack animals for thousands of years. The alpacas—well, Lilly, you might not like that—but the alpacas are used for their meat and fur. They make the softest yarn for wool shawls," said Maximo. He glanced at Lilly, remembering her feelings about the cuyes.

Luckily for him, Mrs. Curador and the doctors entered the room and interrupted their talk about animal rights. Just one look at their faces and the kids knew: no llamas had been found that night. Their smart plan didn't work.

"So..." said Mr. Cook, shaking his head. "No llamas. No empty treat bowls, except for the nibbling of some small rat-like creatures that enjoyed the salad and apples that Lilly put in there."

That must have been the wild chinchillas. Fynn thought fondly of his furry friend from the day before.

"I really thought we created a good perimeter around the ruins. If the llamas wandered off site but stayed close for shelter, they would've had to pass by one of the treat bowls. Animals are always motivated by hunger and the search for food," said Mrs. Cook.

"And there were no new tracks or droppings in any of the outside areas we searched," said Mr. Cook.

"This can only mean that the herd has moved on," said Mrs. Curador sadly. "Maybe it's time for us to accept that the llamas of Machu Picchu are gone."

"Mom! No!" Maximo cried out angrily.

Lily! Where are you? Why did you leave? Human Lilly's eyes filled with tears. Would she not get the chance to meet her adorable namesake?

CHAPTER 13

After delivering the disastrous news, the adults left to write up an official report in Mrs. Curador's office. The Cook children joined together around Maximo, who was slumped in a chair.

"What can we do?" asked Fynn desperately.

"I can't give up on the herd," said Maximo. "They are my friends. I can't just accept that they're gone. I can't just replace friends. Why doesn't Mom understand? Please help me!"

"Oh, Maximo!" said Celia sadly. She could totally understand how he felt right now. "We'll do whatever we can while we're still here. Maybe we can go out even farther today?"

"And I know what else we're going to do while we're still here," said Lilly with determination. "We will free those two guinea pigs from the kitchen!"

"Lilly! Can you please let it go?" said her brother. "They eat guinea pigs in

Peru. Is it weird for us? Yes! But it's their culture, and we're the visitors here. May I remind you about US President Garfield? Do you still remember what his favorite meal was?" He looked at his sister.

Fynn had received a book about presidential pets for his eighth birthday and loved quoting strange facts about US presidents from it.

"Squirrel soup," Lilly said quietly.

"Presidential squirrel soup!" Fynn repeated in a loud voice.

"It's ok," said Maximo suddenly. "I understand. It's important to you, like it's important to me to find the llamas. I'll help you to free your two pets tonight." He shrugged and smiled at Lilly.

"Thank you, thank you, thank you! Maximo, you're the best!" said Lilly, jumping up from her seat. "With your help, we can sneak into the kitchen later and open their cage. If someone sees us, we'll simply pretend that we're collecting some more treats for the llamas. And tomorrow we'll go out and look for the herd all day long. We must have missed some clues out there."

"I hate to interrupt your genius plan," said Celia, "but do you guys remember what Dad said? Cuyes aren't found in the wild anymore up here. What are you going to do with your rescued pets, Lilly?"

"Well, I wouldn't be so sure about that," said Fynn. He told his sisters all about the wild chinchilla he had seen by the outer rock walls of the ruins. "Chinchillas and guinea pigs aren't that different in their needs. I'm pretty sure the pair of cuyes would be able to survive up here."

"Your dad did say they're not found in the wild *anymore*. That means they must have been native at one point," admitted Maximo, coming to his rescue.

"So, it's decided?" asked Lilly.

"First we rescue the cuyes. Then we save the llamas."

All three heads nodded in agreement. They had a plan!

CHAPTER 14

Fynn and his sisters were awoken by soft tapping on their hotel bedroom door.

"It's me," whispered Maximo from outside.

"Operation cuy, go!" said Fynn sleepily.

They dressed quickly and met Maximo outside their door. Using only soft whispers and hand gestures, the kids made their way down the stairs. When they turned to enter the big dining room that led to the kitchen, Maximo held up his palms and motioned them to a small door on the right.

"Let's use this way," he said. "They might be setting up for breakfast in the dining room already."

They nodded and squeezed into the tight hallway behind the door he had pointed at. Lilly could hear their own rapid exhales in the small space.

Suddenly, she detected another

sound: soft squeaking voices from the end of the hallway. *We're coming for you,* she thought.

They all came to a stop before the kitchen door. "Fynn, you and Celia should stay here to guard the hallway, ok?" Maximo said quietly.

Fynn nodded and turned around to keep an eye on the dark hallway behind him. Lilly took a deep breath and pushed the door handle down. The opening door didn't make a sound, but the kitchen behind it was filled with frantic squeaking and scratching noises.

"Guinea pigs are most active during the night," she said, turning to

Maximo. "Let's get them out of their cage and into the wild quickly."

The boy headed to the counter where the small cage was kept. He slowly opened the latched door and reached inside to grab the animals.

"Ouch! These beasts!!" he screamed and pulled his hand back instantly. He brought his index finger up to his face and saw small blood drops forming on it.

"They bit me!" he said to Lilly.

"Here, let me," said Lilly calmly. Her instincts as the daughter of two

veterinarians took over. She grabbed a clean paper towel from the counter behind her and gently wrapped it around Maximo's bleeding finger.

"It's just a tiny wound. Hold it up for a bit," she reassured the boy.

Lilly headed back to the cage and crouched down to look through the open wire door. The two animals were huddled up in the far back corner, shaking violently. *They probably think we are here to roast them,* Lilly thought, horrified.

She slowly reached both her open palms inside the cage and murmured calm words to the guinea pigs. When she was sure that the animals were less afraid, she quickly turned her hands up and grabbed both of them with a well-practiced movement on the thickest part of their bodies, just behind their heads.

"Gotcha!" she said happily. *All that hamster wrestling at home has paid off,* she thought as she held the chubby creatures close to her body.

CHAPTER 15

At this moment, Fynn and Celia burst through the door. "Someone's coming down the hallway!" said Fynn urgently. "We have to go!"

"This way!" said Maximo, pointing at the main door. "There's no choice. We must risk going back through the dining hall."

He was still holding his bleeding finger, wrapped tightly with a paper towel.

"What happened?" asked Fynn.

"Revenge of the cuyes," said Maximo. "Probably well deserved. I'll tell you everything later. Let's go before we get caught!"

The large kitchen door had just gently closed behind the four children and two guinea pigs when they heard the humming sound of the lights being turned on behind them.

As they hurried through the dark room toward the exit to the patio, Celia

recognized a familiar, bear-like voice coming from the kitchen.

"Chef Chuchu!" she said anxiously. *How long will it take my cooking teacher to discover that his prized cuyes are gone?* she wondered. What will he do when he finds out? She pushed forward toward the door that would lead them outside and the guinea pigs to freedom.

Lilly crossed the patio all the way to the large stone wall overlooking the ruins below. The moonlight shone on the soft field of grass sloping down from where she was standing with the guinea pigs cradled against her.

"Perfect!" Lilly said.

She cautiously placed the pair into a small nook in the rock wall. "Be free! Be safe!" Lilly whispered. She sent her rescued cuyes off into the night, wishing them a better life in the wild than in a cage in the hotel kitchen.

"Thanks again, Maximo!" she said, turning back to the other kids, who had stood back silently. "I'm sorry the cuyes didn't appreciate your rescue more. I

really think we did the right thing here. And I promise we'll find Lily and her llama friends for you next. We're the Cook kids after all!"

CHAPTER 16

It felt like they had barely slept when Fynn and Maximo left the hotel in the morning, this time through the front doors. They headed straight to the ruins to continue their training before the constant streams of visitors clogged their way.

After a couple of stretches, the boys took off running. Maximo led his friend to a new part of the Inca path toward some of the old rope bridges.

"The ancient engineers built these so well that some of the bridges are still hanging between the canyons," Maximo explained. "Nobody's allowed to use them any longer, but they're really cool to see!"

As they ran past the more popular areas of the ruins, Fynn kept bumping into some early rising tourists here and there.

"I can't believe they're up here already," he mumbled angrily to himself, dodging a family to his right.

"Where are the llamas, Mom?" they heard a girl complain in English. "I promised Jess I'd post a selfie with one later today."

Fynn could not hear the answer because Maximo pulled him away and continued their run upward and away from the tourists.

They had just left one of the main outer walls behind when Maximo stopped suddenly and let out a surprised squeal.

"Fynn!" he said, grabbing his friend's shoulder. "Are those the cuyes?"

"How on earth?" Fynn said. "If there aren't any wild guinea pigs in the ruins, these must be ours. They've come a long way since last night. Let's see what they're up to, ok? Lilly won't believe this!"

The boys ran after the two small animals. The cuyes were scurrying at a fast pace, and they hurried up to follow them.

Up and down the path they went, suddenly turning into an overgrown part of the trail.

First I'm training with an Inca runner, now I'm training with guinea pigs, thought Fynn. He shook his head in disbelief and ran into the bushes with Maximo close by his side.

After a couple of strides, they came to a halt. The guinea pigs had dashed into a tight opening of a rock formation that stretched out in front of them. The massive rock pile reached far above the boys' heads.

"Do you know where we are?" asked Fynn.

"I'm not sure. I don't think I've been down this way," said Maximo. "The mountain still moves and sometimes rocks fall down or plants grow over parts of the trails. No, I don't recognize it."

They moved closer to the opening and tried to peek inside. As they approached, they both heard a soft humming sound from inside the rocks.

"It seems like it goes farther in. There must be a cave inside," said Fynn.

"Do you know what makes humming sounds?" asked Maximo as his face lit up. "Llamas singing to their babies!"

"No way!" said Fynn. *Can this be it?* he thought. "We have to get Lilly and Celia. I think we found the llamas!"

CHAPTER 17

"So, let me get this straight," said Celia. "You saw the guinea pigs out in the wild. Then you found the missing llamas. And all this, while Lilly and I were eating breakfast and listening to Chef Chuchu's theories about the runaway cuyes?"

Lilly and Celia looked at the boys, frowning. This was too much!

"Well, we came back for you. Didn't we?" said Fynn. He was just glad they had finally discovered a clue for their friend. "Let's go and find out what's going on in that cave."

Soon all four kids were heading up the steep Inca trails again. Since Celia was complaining nonstop, Fynn and Maximo had slowed their pace to a walk. *Why does my twin hate any type of exercise besides dancing?* wondered Fynn. *Isn't she excited to finally find the llamas?* Fynn couldn't get there soon enough.

They made their way back to the rock formation without any problem. The rescued cuyes were sitting sunbathing on a rock at the entrance, just like two little stone statues.

"My guinea pigs!" exclaimed Lilly. "They're ok!"

As they approached, the two guinea pigs stretched and disappeared into the opening. The children hurried after them. Soft humming noises welcomed them as soon as they got closer to the gap in the rocks.

"Singing llamas!" said Lilly. It was the most wonderful sound she had ever heard. *The herd is safe and happy if it is making these noises!* Lilly thought.

The boys started squeezing their bodies sideways through the small slit. They motioned back to Lilly and Celia to follow them. After a short, tight passage, the rock formation opened into a comfortable cave. A couple of narrow passages led in different directions.

"I don't think we should go much farther without flashlights," said Maximo.

"Listen!" said Lilly. She took a couple of steps closer to a passage on her left. When she got closer, she could hear soft voices and see some beams of sunshine bouncing off the dark stone walls.

The kids crowded together and quietly listened to the sound of different animals humming and cooing. There were deeper booming voices and small timid voices speaking up from time to time. Lilly could almost picture a herd of llamas in all shapes and sizes huddled together in a large underground cave.

She wondered if Lily the llama was among them and what her adorable voice sounded like.

Suddenly, a loud and shrill noise interrupted the beautiful humming. Everything else stopped as the kids heard a raspy scream, "Mwa, mwa!" over and over again. It echoed off the narrow passage walls turning into an eerie shriek.

"Quick! Let's get out of here!" said Maximo with urgency in his voice. "We've been discovered. That's the llamas' alarm call!"

CHAPTER 18

"Phew," said Fynn, and he plopped into his usual chair in the Sanctuary's dining room. "First we didn't find the llamas, and now I felt like I was being chased by a herd of wild llamas."

"Even Celia made a run for it!" said Lilly, laughing.

"What about me?" asked Celia as she entered the room. She was balancing a big plate of tortilla chips and a bowl of the local green salsa, courtesy of Chef Chuchu.

"We were just discussing your speed coming down the mountain," said her brother, never missing a chance to annoy his twin.

Celia, however, wasn't in the mood for joking. She was simply confused about their discovery. Why were the llamas hiding in a cave? How did they even get food and water there? Why had they chosen to leave their usual home, the beautiful green fields of Machu Picchu?

The kids dug into the bowl of fresh chips and salsa. The sound of crunching

 was the only noise in the big room for a long time.

"I don't understand this," said Maximo finally, speaking what they were all thinking. "Why would the entire herd be hiding in a cave of all places?"

"There are no new predators. The food and water sources are the same and not poisoned," Lilly counted down reasons on her fingers. "The visitors have been coming here..."

"Of course!" said Fynn, slapping his hand on his forehead. "The visitors! Lilly, you got it!"

Maximo and the girls looked at each other in surprise. Maybe Fynn had been running up and down Machu Picchu too much today? He didn't make sense to any of them.

"Listen for a moment, guys!" said Fynn, holding up both hands. "Remember how everyone keeps telling us that the number of tourists to Machu Picchu has grown so much in the past years? And remember how the people we heard in the ruins all wanted to see the llamas and take selfies with them?" The other kids nodded.

"That made me think of the time when Mom and Dad hosted the open house at home." He turned to Maximo.

"A lot of visitors came to the clinic to meet our vet parents and hear about their famous adventures healing animals around the world. They all visited our chicken run, the fish pond, and the goats in the back. Our goats love attention, and they'll do anything for treats, so we thought they were having a blast."

"Toward the end of the afternoon, a little girl came running and told me that the goats had disappeared. I followed her back, and she was right—no goat in sight, even though there were tons of people at the fence ready with their treat bags."

At this point in the story, he reached for the bowl, took another chip, and chewed it slowly.

"Fynn!" said his sisters, glaring at him with exactly the same expression. Now Lilly and Celia looked like twins!

"Okay, okay! So anyway, the people and treats were there, the goats were gone. What had happened was that the four goats had apparently had enough of the people outside their fence and had squeezed into the hay barn, which is separated from their usual sleeping place. There they were, munching on their hay and dozing in the peace and quiet."

"You're absolutely right, Lilly. I don't think the visitors have changed, but their numbers sure have!" Fynn finished his conclusion with a bang.

Maximo nodded along in agreement. The girls looked at each other and grinned. It seemed that their brother had put the missing pieces together.

"That's great! Only, now we have the usual problem," said Celia. "How will we convince our parents and Mrs. Curador that they need to let in fewer visitors to bring back the llamas of Machu Picchu?"

CHAPTER 19

"Mom!" Maximo stormed into Mrs. Curador's office with the Cook kids trailing right behind him. They had opted for the direct approach with their parents.

"You've got to give the llamas one more chance!" he said without missing a beat.

His mom sighed. She looked at the doctors pleadingly.

"Maximo, sweetie, we're so sorry. We don't think there is anything else we can try," said Mrs. Cook. "Believe me, it's so hard for us to come all this way and not be able to help you more."

"But we think we still can!" said Fynn. "You know, we were just talking about how our goats went into hiding during the open house back home. People kept shoving treats at them and taking pictures. We thought there were too many visitors that day, and the animals wanted to relax without being disturbed. Remember that, Dad?"

"And then, we talked to Chef Chuchu in the kitchen, who was telling us about how much quieter the ruins used to be.

He said that the number of tourists keeps growing every year, even every month," said Lilly.

"We're kind of wondering if the llamas are hiding because there are simply too many people around right now," said Celia, finishing their explanation.

"Like they reached the point of **exodus...**" mumbled Mr. Cook while he looked at the other two adults. They all seemed deep in thought, considering the kids' story.

"What does that even mean, Dad?" asked Celia.

"They needed to leave the area

because outside factors, in this case, the people, were forcing them to move on," said Mrs. Cook. "If this is the case, their own popularity with the tourists has driven the llamas away."

"I guess it's worth a try?" said Mr. Cook.

Maximo's mom sighed. "That's going to be hard to explain. The visitors have traveled from far to see the famous ruins. Oh well, I guess we might be able to start a trial for the rest of the  week and give the herd a chance to return. If they are still around," she said.

"I bet they are!" exclaimed Celia, and she winked at the other kids. They had done it! The llamas would get another chance to return home.

CHAPTER 20

The next day was a blur of activity around the Sanctuary offices. As promised, Mrs. Curador and her team started to create plans for limiting entry to the ruins for the rest of the week. This was a massive job and not something that could be introduced hastily. The doctors helped them by researching and writing reports about the effects of mass tourism on the wildlife.

The four kids kept busy in their own way. Celia had moved into the kitchen where she worked with Chef Chuchu. While she filled her notebook with recipes from Peru, she also tried to give him ideas for festive meals that did not include any guinea pigs. *Worth a try,* she thought.

Maximo continued to push Fynn with his Inca runner's training. They made their way to different parts of the Inca trail several times per day. Soon Fynn matched the Peruvian boy's smooth rhythm and felt better and better running in the high altitude and on the winding paths.

And Lilly? She was the only one who secretly visited the cave of the llamas while everyone else was working on their return. She couldn't get over the soft humming and hoped to finally catch a glimpse of Lily, her long lost llama friend. Every time she returned to the rock formation, the rescued cuyes were ready for her and walked into the cave to listen to the llamas with her.

On her last evening visit, she brought along a flashlight to go farther down the path on the left. Her guinea pig buddies stayed close as she carefully stepped over rocks. Suddenly, her foot touched something soft. *Grass?* Lilly was surprised.

As she cautiously peeked around the next corner, the sight took her breath away. A large, open cavern with bushes and grassy spots stretched out in front of her. The space was lit by natural sunshine coming from several gaping holes in the rocks. Water trickled down the stone walls into a natural basin. And there they were. Lilly glimpsed a herd of soft wooly creatures standing loosely together in a far corner.

They are as beautiful as I have imagined them all this time, she thought dreamily as she slowly backed out of the cave.

"There must be another way in," she told her siblings and Maximo after her return. They had given her a hard time when she admitted that she had continued to visit the llamas without them. "That would explain how the herd could have been in

hiding for so long without even coming out to nibble on our treat bowls."

"It's like in your story!" said Maximo. "Your goats were hiding in the hay barn, and my llamas are hiding in an underground shelter."

"I can't wait until they come outside again," said Celia.

Their patience was soon rewarded. In the evening, Mrs. Curador met her son and the Cook family in the dining hall for an announcement.

"Tomorrow is the big day," she said, beaming. "The first trial of timed entrance slots at Machu Picchu. This system will be good for everyone, tourists and missing llamas alike. The visitors will be able to better admire the beauty of the ruins. Our wildlife will be less disturbed."

"Maybe this will even bring the chinchillas closer to the ruins," said Fynn.

"Let's start working on the llamas first," said his dad. "I'm not so sure if our plan will make a difference for them at this point."

CHAPTER 21

Everyone got up early in the morning. The excitement was buzzing in the room at breakfast and at the gates to the ruins when they headed over. Fynn nudged his sisters and pointed at the orderly lines that had been formed. Each guard was standing next to a sign with large numbers, showing the current time slots for people allowed to enter Machu Picchu.

Lilly overheard a woman wearing a head scarf explaining to her friend,  "They're trying to organize it better now, I guess. I'm so happy we got the first visiting time this morning. We might be able to see the native animals."

See, they get it. They understand why this is important, thought Lilly happily.

Once they made their way into the city, Mrs. Curador joined them.

"I'm surprised by how positive the visitors are already! No complaints so far.

We've had a couple of little mistakes, but that was to be expected with so many people. If this trial works out, we might be able to move the entire entrance system to digital timed passes."

"Just like at the Empire State Building," said Celia. Their parents had taken them to visit this famous site in New York not too long ago. She still remembered how they had to enter the building and the elevator at a certain time. "We didn't have to wait in line at all when we went. I thought it was brilliant!" she told Maximo.

"The people are happy. Now it'll hopefully also make the llamas happy so they can return," he said.

Their small group continued to walk the city throughout the day, always on the lookout for some furry creatures in the distance. By late afternoon, the crowds were still not as large as they had been the days before.

"Nobody has stepped on my toes yet!" said Celia happily.

"But still no llamas!" said Mrs. Cook. "I wonder if they wandered too far already and won't realize it's safe to return."

That's it! Lilly grabbed Maximo's arm tightly. "Mom, can we check out one of the Inca trails that Maximo wanted to show us before we leave?"

Barely waiting for the answer, she took off, pulling the boy behind her and telling her siblings to follow along.

She only stopped when they came to the rock formation, safely hiding the herd of llamas from view. The usual soft humming and two sunbathing guinea pigs were expecting them.

Lilly got closer slowly and knelt down beside the pair. "Hi there, cuties! Today, I'm not going in. I need you to bring out the llamas. We've taken care of their problem, just like we took care of yours. They'll be able to move around in peace now," she whispered to the cuyes.

"What's your sister doing?" asked Maximo, his dark eyes widening.

"Talking to your escaped dinner," said Fynn with a straight face. They had experienced so many curious adventures with animals around the world. His sister talking to guinea pigs rescued from the cooking pot didn't surprise him at all.

CHAPTER 22

"It's getting late, guys. Let's call it a day!" said Fynn. He sat with his back leaned against a large stone. Celia and Lilly were stretched out in the grass next to him. Of course, Maximo was bouncing up and down the path in his usual way.

They had waited at the rock formation for ages. Sadly, neither the cuyes nor the llamas, nor the cuyes riding the llamas had appeared.

They caught up to their parents standing at the large stone wall where Fynn and Maximo had first placed the llama treat bowls. The adults all stared into the distance gloomily.

"At least the entrance system was a success," said Mrs. Curador. "I'm just sad that we'll never find out what happened to our llamas."

"I'm so sorry we couldn't solve this case," said Mrs. Cook, pulling the kids into a hug. "Let's enjoy one more gorgeous sunset over the city in the clouds before we start thinking about heading home tomorrow."

"What? Hey! Whoa...look!" cried Mr. Cook, gesturing wildly into the sunset beyond the Inca walls. "I could've sworn I saw a pair of cuyes scurrying along the rocks over there."

 "Dad!" said Lilly, hardly able to keep a straight face. "There are no wild guinea pigs in Machu Picchu. Remember, you told us so!"

Maximo and Fynn were bursting

with laughter. Celia had to turn around to hide her face from her dad.

"But I really thought...I saw...And two of them!" Mr. Cook babbled.

"Oh my!" screamed Celia at that moment. She was pointing in the direction she had turned. "You saw llamas, Dad!"

They all shifted their eyes to the most beautiful sight they had ever seen. Hundreds of cameras and phones started clicking and flashing around them. Everyone turned silent and seemed to hold their breaths.

Just beyond the last Inca stone wall with its perfectly placed rock pieces, the

shapes of a large herd of llamas moved slowly toward the ancient ruins of Machu Picchu. The sinking sun dipped the background in an orange glow. The last sun rays caught the wooly white and brown fur of the llamas, shining brightly like magical creatures.

This, right here, should be a painting, thought Celia.

"Your llamas certainly know how to make an entrance," said Fynn to Maximo.

"Well, they kept their audience waiting for a long time." His friend smiled. He felt the warm glow of the sunset. *My llamas are safe! And even better, they have returned to their home!*

Lilly squinted at the herd walking in the distance. One, two, five, ten...where was she? Finally, at the very end of the line, a huge friendly face turned toward her. She was sure she heard a soft humming noise that was just meant for her. *Llama Lily! It is so nice to finally meet you!*

CHAPTER 23

It had been a long night of celebrations at the Sanctuary. Everyone was congratulating the doctors and Mrs. Curador on the return of the lost llamas. The kitchen door kept banging open with Chef Chuchu bringing out platters of delicious dishes. None of them included cuyes though, as Celia said to Lilly in between two bites.

Since the children were all packed and had said their goodbyes to their new friends at the Sanctuary, their parents agreed to let them go back to the ruins one more time the next morning.

"It was great finding the llamas. It was even better bringing them home. But now I really want to see them up close, too!" said Lilly to Maximo.

The atmosphere at the upper fields had changed completely from the days before. Chatty tourists strolled along the paths, admiring the llamas grazing in the grass beyond the wall. Little kids ran up to the border, excitedly pointing at the peaceful herd.

A girl their age posed for a selfie, positioning her phone to catch the perfect shot of the llama in the background. A couple of the animals walked up to the wall, getting close to the small group of visitors. They almost seemed to enjoy having their pictures taken with their human fans.

Lilly was admiring the peaceful scene when a large buck-toothed head appeared over the wall she had rested her arms on.

"Tag number twenty-three," read Maximo. "Lilly, meet Lily!"

Without hesitation, Lilly held out her palm, and the llama's soft nose lightly brushed her hand. Huge dark eyes framed by beautiful long lashes looked into her human eyes. *What a special moment,* she thought.

"Smile!" said Celia, interrupting the magic. "This picture will be great!"

CHAPTER 24

Celia was not looking forward to retracing their steps all the way home to the United States. She had truly enjoyed the beauty—and the food—of Machu Picchu. What she had not enjoyed was the long journey, which started with the stomach-turning bus ride down the mountain. She sighed and put on her headphones, pumping up the volume on her phone. In her mind, she was already back home, dancing at her long-awaited ballet recital. It felt like she hadn't had a chance to think about her music since their adventures with the dancing horses in Austria.

"So then you run the last distance as fast as you can. Don't save any more energy, ok?" Maximo was giving Fynn final instructions on how to win his race back home.

"Email me a picture of the medal," he said, grinning.

"I will!" The boys bumped their fists, and Fynn climbed onto the bus, waving back at his new friend. He felt

confident that the training of the Inca runners would help him win his race. After all, the chasquis were the greatest runners in the world at one time. He felt lucky to have trained with one of their own descendants in Peru. He would really miss his running partner, Maximo.

Lilly held a miniature llama tightly in her hand. Mrs. Curador had given each of them a small toy, spun out of real alpaca fur. It was as soft as a cloud.

"These are for the good luck to follow you back home," she had said to Lilly, wrapping her in a warm embrace.

Lilly leaned back and let her mind wander to llama Lily and her herd.

Then she thought of the guinea pigs they had rescued together with their new friend. She somehow knew they would have a happy life in the wild.

What a crazy adventure this has been, she thought. Who would have thought that some escaped guinea pigs would help them solve the case of the lost llamas? But then again, who would have thought that horses would talk to them in Austria or dogs would bark in her head in New York City.

Lilly sat up straight. She had a brilliant idea: someone needed to write down their adventures! And this was the perfect time to get started. Their trip back home would take forever anyway.

Yes, Lilly thought excitedly, *I know just where to begin.*

The place to start telling their story was definitely beginning with the wild dogs in Central Park. She still remembered the morning her parents had received a frantic email.

The assistant of the mayor in New York City had urgently needed their help...

VISITING MACHU PICCHU TODAY

During the era of the Incas, Machu Picchu housed only 1,000 people. Nowadays, more than 1.2 million tourists visit this famous site every year.

In the year 2017, the government of Peru introduced a timed ticketing system, limiting the visitors to 2,500 per day.

All visitors are required to enter with a special guide.

It is not allowed to walk into roped-off areas or to take rocks from the ruins.

Visitors are asked to carry out their own trash and avoid plastic.

GLOSSARY

Peru: Peru is a country on the west coast of South America. Today, the city of Lima is Peru's capital. During the time of the Incas, Cuzco, a city high up in the mountains, was Peru's capital. As it has many different kinds of landscapes and types of weather, Peru is home to over 20,000 different kinds of plants and animals.

Camelids: These animals are large plant eaters with slender necks and long legs. Their upper lips are split into two mobile parts. They do not have hooves, but two-toed feet with toenails and soft pads ideal for walking on rocks. Camels, llamas, alpacas, and vicuñas all belong to this family.

Llama: The large, wooly llama with its different colors is from South America. People in Peru have used these friendly animals for thousands of years to help them move things high up in the mountains. These animals eat grass, need little water, and do well with the high, thin air of the Andes Mountains. Llamas can kick or spit chewed food if they feel threatened. When they are happy, they often run and bounce. A small herd still roams the ancient ruins of Machu Picchu and poses for pictures with visitors.

Alpaca: Peru is home to about 90 percent of the alpacas in the world. They live in large herds mostly in the valleys. Due to their smaller size, they are not used as pack animals but for their meat and fluffy fur. Alpacas come in over twenty-two different colors.

Vicuña: These animals live wild in Peru and other South American countries. Vicuñas are smaller and shier than llamas and alpacas. Their soft wool is the most valuable. They are a protected endangered species.

Machu Picchu (machoo-peechoo): Literally, "Old Mountain." Machu Picchu was the winter palace built by the Inca King **Pachacuti** high up in the mountains of Peru. It offered protection from enemies and a perfect view of the sun, which was holy for the Incas. The ancient city is a wonder of engineering and farming. The Incas built terraces for crops and constructed houses and temples made of stone and wood. They had aqueducts carrying pure water through the city and a large system of trails. Machu Picchu was designed to blend into nature. It was lost after the fall of the Inca Empire and found in 1911 by **Hiram Bingham.** Today, it is one of the most beloved sites in the world.

Quechua (cat-chew-ah): This was the language spoken by the ancient Inca. It is still used by many people in Peru today, even though their official language is Spanish. Fun fact: in Quechua, the word "Inca" means "King."

Incas: In the 1400s, a tribe in South America became very powerful. They called themselves "Inca." The people were talented engineers, builders, farmers, and artists. They studied the stars and planets. Incas built many strong cities, such as Machu Picchu, and grew their empire. When the Spanish discovered and invaded South America, the Incas tried to protect their way of living. They were not successful. By the year 1572, the last of the Inca Empire and their culture were gone.

Bienvenidos: Spanish for "welcome."

Señora: Spanish for "Mrs."

Anthropologist: When you become an anthropologist, you study the lives of humans and their cultures in the past and present. There are many different special fields of anthropology.

Plantains: Bananas used for cooking. They are popular in South American kitchens.

Civilization: A group of people with a certain culture and way of life in a specific area is called a civilization.

Tourism: When you travel for business or fun to a place outside your home, you become a tourist. Tourism is an important way to earn money for many people and countries. It has many positive effects but can also cause problems like pollution and overcrowding.

Pachacuti (puch-ah-kootee): He was an Inca king who built Machu Picchu as a winter home and made the Inca Empire bigger by fighting and making deals with other tribes. His name meant "Earth Shaker." Pachacuti wore a puma skin on his head when he went into battle. He died before the Spanish took over the cities he built.

Cuchillo: Spanish for "knife."

Buenos dias: Spanish for "hello!" Literally, "good day!"

One cuy, two cuyes: Spanish for "guinea pig."

Hiram Bingham: This explorer was born in 1875 in Hawaii. He was sent to study at **Yale University** in Connecticut, where he became a professor of South Amercan history as an adult. In 1908, he traveled to South America for the first timc. In 1911, he made his big discovery when he stumbled over the ruins of Machu Picchu and showed them to the world. The movie *Indiana Jones* might be based on Hiram Bingham, a professor turned jungle explorer.

The Andes: This mountain range runs along South America's western side and is one of the world's longest ranges. The Andes have glaciers, volcanoes, grasslands, deserts, lakes, and forests.

Chasquis (tchas-kiss): These runners were the mailmen of the Inca Empire. They ran on the steep, rocky paths the Incas built to connect their cities throughout the Andes Mountains. The runners worked by a relay system: one roadrunner would carry a message down the road and tell it to the next roadrunner. They sounded conch shells to alert the runner after them.

Viscacha (vis-catchuh): These animals are closely related to chinchillas but built slightly larger. They resemble rabbits with longer bushy tails and furry ears. These creatures are native to the Andes in Peru. They are also known for their very soft fur. Like chinchillas, they live in large families and prefer harsh rocky environments high in the mountains.

Exodus: A mass departure of people or animals due to outside factors.

ABOUT THE AUTHOR

Dori Marx grew up in Austria and traveled the world several times before choosing New England as her home. Here, she lives with her husband, three children, and a senior dog, along with an ever-growing number of rescue goats, pet chickens, and fish. Although she isn't a vet, she has a soft spot for all living beings and has even learned to coexist with the spiders in her basement.

Dori's books are illustrated by artists living in the countries that the Wonder World Kids visit. These local illustrators lend their unique style to the artwork for each book.

The Case of the Lost Llamas is the second book in her *Wonder World Kids Series*.

Made in the USA
Monee, IL
08 March 2021

62194642R00111